Caroline and the Yellow Cat

Chris Riddell, Children's Laureate 2015–2017, is an accomplished artist and political cartoonist for the *Observer*. His books have won many awards, including the Kate Greenaway Medal, the Nestlé Children's Book Prize and the Red House Children's Book Award. *Goth Girl and the Ghost of a Mouse* won the Costa Children's Book Award in 2013.

Chris RIDDELL

Ottoline
and the
Yellow Cat

MACMILLAN CHILDREN'S BOOKS

For my daughter, Katy

Chapter One

Ottoline lived on the twenty-fourth floor of the Pepperpot Building. It was called the P. W. HUFFLEDINCK Tower but it looked just like a pepper pot so everyone called it the Pepperpot Building.

THE PEPPERPOT BUILDING

APARTMENT 243

THE SHOEBOX BUILDING

THE POINTY TOWER

THE ICECREAM CONE BUILDING

THE CLOWN'S HAT BUILDING

THE PAUL STEWART III BUILDING

GRUBERMAN'S KOREAN THEATRE

LIKES SPLASHING IN PUDDLES AND COLLECTING THINGS

Ottoline

Mr. Munroe

SMALL, HAIRY AND FROM A BOG IN NORWAY

She lived in Apartment 243 with Mr. Munroe, who was small and hairy and didn't like the rain or having his hair brushed.

Ottoline, on the other hand, loved all kinds of weather, particularly rain, because she liked splashing in puddles. She also liked brushing Mr. Munroe's hair. She found it very relaxing, and it helped her to think, especially if there was a tricky problem to solve or a clever plan to work out.

Ottoline liked solving tricky problems and working out clever plans even more than she liked splashing in puddles. She kept her eyes and ears open in case she came across anything unusual or interesting. So did Mr. Munroe.

Ottoline's parents travelled the world collecting interesting things. Apartment 243 was full of the things that they collected.

EMPERORS' HATS

METEORITES

SEASHELLS

EXTREMELY SMALL PAINTINGS

SNUFF BOTTLES

HOT-WATER BOTTLES

BLUE BOTTLES

BUTTERFLY COLLECTORS' NETS

MASKS

PARROT CLOCKS

PORTABLE FISHBOWLS

LEAKING CUPS

Her parents had promised that one day, when she was older, Ottoline could join them on their travels, but until then she was to stay at home and look after their collections.

Ottoline didn't mind too much because she had Mr. Munroe for company.

MYSTERIOUS OBJECTS OF VARIOUS KINDS

One day, while out for an afternoon stroll, Mr. Munroe noticed a poster stuck to a lamp post outside Gruberman's Korean Theatre. He carefully peeled it off and folded it up. Then he put it under his arm, as, being small and hairy, Mr. Munroe didn't have any pockets. He took it home with him.

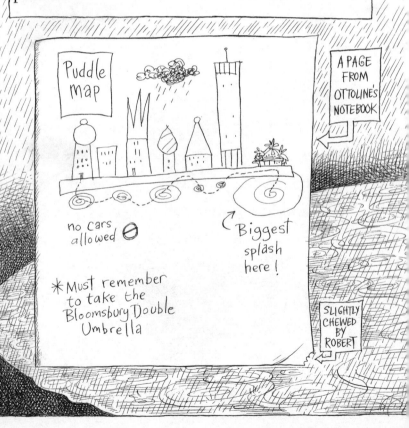

Puddle map

no cars allowed

Biggest splash here!

*Must remember to take the Bloomsbury Double Umbrella

A PAGE FROM OTTOLINE'S NOTEBOOK

SLIGHTLY CHEWED BY ROBERT

Later that afternoon, Ottoline was dusting
the four-spouted teapot collection when she
felt a tap on her shoulder. It was Mr. Munroe.
He showed her the poster from the lamp post
outside Gruberman's Korean Theatre.

lost

A Penangese lapdog
answers to the name
Rupert Pom-Pom Fluffy-Tail

Much missed by his loving owner

large Reward

CONTACT: Mrs. Loretta Lloyd, Apartment 11112,
The Clown's Hat Building, 3rd st., B.C.

ARMPIT
HAIR

"How interesting," Ottoline said. "You don't have any more of these, by any chance?"

Mr. Munroe went to his room. It was very untidy.

When he came back, Ottoline was reorganizing her Odd Shoe collection.

Ottoline had two collections that were all her own. One was her Odd Shoe collection, of which she was very proud. Whenever Ottoline bought a pair of shoes, she would wear one and put the other in her collection.

IF YOU'D LIKE TO FIND OUT ABOUT OTTOLINE'S OTHER COLLECTION, TURN TO PAGE 45

SOME OF OTTOLINE'S ODD SHOES

Mr. Munroe showed Ottoline the posters he'd
collected from lamp posts all over town.

Ottoline looked at them for a long time.
"I don't suppose . . ." she said, "you'd let me
brush your hair?"

While she brushed Mr. Munroe's hair, Ottoline looked more closely at the posters.

THIS IS WHAT OTTOLINE LOOKS LIKE WHEN SHE'S THINKING OF A CLEVER PLAN

WILSON HAPPY-EARS McMURTAGH

COUNT OLTO VIX-HILBURG

FIFI FIESTA FUNNY-FACE III

That evening Ottoline and Mr. Munroe sat
down to dinner. Ottoline had grilled cheese and
cinnamon toast freshly delivered to the table by

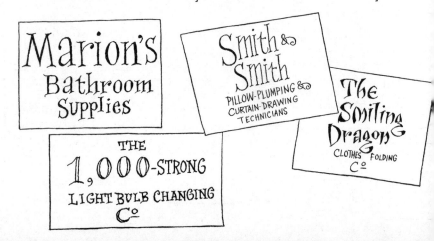

Marion's
Bathroom
Supplies

Smith &
Smith
PILLOW-PLUMPING &
CURTAIN-DRAWING
TECHNICIANS

The
Smiling
Dragon
CLOTHES FOLDING
C°

THE
1,000-STRONG
LIGHT BULB CHANGING
C°

the Home-Cooked Meal Company. Mr. Munroe
had a bowl of porridge and a mug of hot
chocolate, which was the only meal he ever ate.

Happy Nest
BED MAKERS

THE
HOME-COOKED
MEAL C°

MB
McBEAN'S CLEANING
SERVICE

Mr. Munroe

D.H.S.
DOOR HANDLE
SHINERS
INC.

OTTOLINE'S
PARENTS WERE
AWAY A LOT,
TRAVELLING, BUT
THEY MADE SURE
OTTOLINE
WAS WELL
LOOKED AFTER
BY LOTS AND
LOTS OF PEOPLE.
THESE ARE
THEIR BUSINESS
CARDS

After dinner, Ottoline went down to the
laundry room in the basement of the
Pepperpot Building.

Ottoline liked to do her own laundry for
two reasons. Firstly, she liked the washing
machines . . .

And secondly, she liked standing on tiptoe and listening to the pipes in the basement ceiling. Ottoline could hear lots of interesting conversations that went on in other apartments. She didn't tell Mr. Munroe as she knew he wouldn't approve.
... HUGE NUMBERS OF APPLES BUT NOT A SINGLE PEAR, NOT EVEN ON SUNDAYS ...
NORMALLY CECIL IS SUCH A GOOD BOY BUT LAST TUESDAY...
...THEN MRS. PASTERNAK'S MONKEY REFUSED TO WEAR HIS SILK PYJAMAS...
BIG CITY
HOT

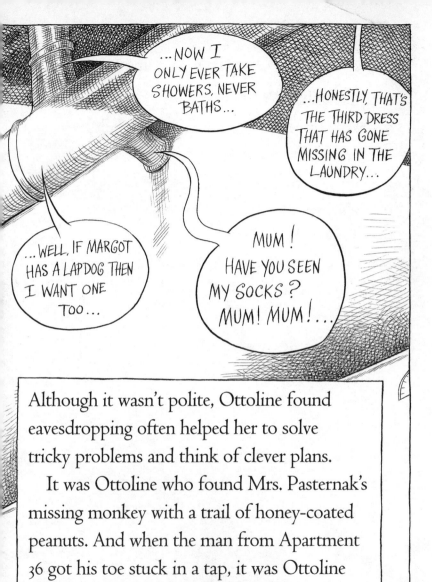

...NOW I ONLY EVER TAKE SHOWERS, NEVER BATHS...

...HONESTLY, THAT'S THE THIRD DRESS THAT HAS GONE MISSING IN THE LAUNDRY...

...WELL, IF MARGOT HAS A LAPDOG THEN I WANT ONE TOO...

MUM! HAVE YOU SEEN MY SOCKS? MUM! MUM!...

Although it wasn't polite, Ottoline found eavesdropping often helped her to solve tricky problems and think of clever plans.

It was Ottoline who found Mrs. Pasternak's missing monkey with a trail of honey-coated peanuts. And when the man from Apartment 36 got his toe stuck in a tap, it was Ottoline who called the fire brigade.

That evening, Ottoline was doing her laundry
and listening to the pipes as usual when
a large, hairy arm appeared from behind
one of the washing machines and grabbed
a pair of Ottoline's stripy socks.

Ottoline peered into the shadows.

It was a bear.

"You ought to be ashamed of
yourself, stealing socks," said
Ottoline.

"So should you, listening
in to other people's
conversations," said
the bear.

"I won't tell,
if you won't,"
said Ottoline.

ROBERT IS
IN THE
HABIT OF
READING
OVER
PEOPLE'S
SHOULDERS

MR. MUNROE IS
IN THE HABIT
OF DROPPING
THE PAGES
HE'S NOT
INTERESTED IN
ON THE FLOOR

M r. Munroe was sitting in the
Beidermeyer armchair reading
the newspaper. Mr. Munroe often read his
newspaper if he had trouble getting to sleep or
had a bad dream about the bog in Norway. He
liked to read the travel section, about holidays
on tropical islands and sunny beaches.

Several pages caught Ottoline's eye.

Ottoline got out a pair of Balinese pinking shears from the scissors collection and carefully cut out several items to put in her notebook. Mr. Munroe didn't notice. He was engrossed in a story about the Gobi Desert, where it hardly ever rains.

IF YOU WOULD LIKE TO SEE THIS PAGE OF OTTOLINE'S NOTEBOOK, TURN THE PAGE

NO NEW LEADS IN SHOEBOX BUILDING BURGLARY

By our crime correspondent

Police remain baffled by the burglary in the Shoebox Building on 3rd Street. Despite extensive enquiries and prolonged investigations, Police Commissioner Ronald Flatfoot admitted, "We remain baffled." The victim of the burglary, Mrs. Rachel Armstrong, was too upset to talk to the *Enquirer* last night but said in a written statement, "I have nothing further to add." Police appealed to the public to be vigilant and on their guard at all times.

Mrs. Rachel Armstrong

BURGLARY AT THE POINTY TOWER BAFFLES POLICE

By our crime correspondent

Police remain baffled by the burglary at the Pointy Tower on 3rd Street. Despite extensive enquiries and prolonged investigations, Police Commissioner Ronald Flatfoot admitted, "We remain baffled." The victim of the burglary, Mrs. Dominica Wilson, was too outraged to talk to the *Enquirer* last night but said in a written statement, "I'm too outraged to talk." Police appealed to the public to be vigilant and on their guard at all times.

Mrs. Dominica Wilson

*These dogs look strangely familiar

Mr. Munroe with a haircut! ←

ANOTHER BURGLARY ON 3RD STREET LEAVES NO CLUES

By our crime correspondent

Mrs. Pinky Neugerbauer

Police were baffled last night by another burglary on 3rd Street. In an audacious cat burglary on an apartment on the fifteenth floor of the Ice-Cream Cone building, jewellery worth quite a lot was stolen. Despite initial enquiries and prolonged investigations, police commissioner Ronald Flatfoot admitted, "We are baffled." The victim of the burglary, Mrs. Pinky Neugerbauer was too shocked to talk to the *Enquirer* last night but said in a written statement, "I'm in shock." Police appealed to the public to be vigilant and on their guard at all times.

* Must investigate this ←

I wonder what has been nibbling my notebook? ↘

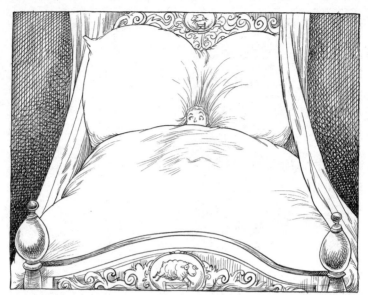

That night, after the Smith & Smith technicians had plumped the pillows and drawn the curtains, Ottoline got out of bed and went to her Special Disguises Wardrobe. Ottoline was a Mistress of Disguise and had a diploma to prove it, from the Who-R-U Academy of Subterfuge.

THIS IS THE DIPLOMA

ACADEMY OF SUBTERFUGE

THIS IS TO CERTIFY THAT

Ottoline Brown

IS A CERTIFIED MISTRESS OF DISGUISE

PROFESSOR MYSTERY M.D.

When she was ready she knocked on
Mr. Munroe's door.

"Your hair could do with a brush," said
Ottoline when he opened the door, "but we
haven't got time for that now. Here, put this
on." She handed Mr. Munroe a large, shabby
raincoat.

Mr. Munroe
handed her an
umbrella just
in case.

They set off through the city.

And very soon were . . .

. . . off the beaten track.

They came to an old warehouse.

Ottoline studied her notebook.

There was a sign on the door which read:

THE LAPDOG
AGENCY

BY APPOINTMENT
ONLY

Mr. Munroe was going to ring the bell
but Ottoline stopped him. Instead they
looked through a rather grubby window.
This is what they saw . . .

The poker players looked strangely familiar. Behind them, a cockatoo was talking into a telephone.

"I'm very sorry, madam, but that's company policy," the cockatoo was saying. "If you lose a lapdog we supplied you with, we can't trust you with another one, now can we? Goodbye."

The cockatoo put the receiver down.

Just then a yellow cat walked in.

"Good evening, boys," she purred. "Had a good week?"

The poker players wagged their tails.

"Excellent," purred the Yellow Cat. "Given Mrs. Neugerbauer the slip, I see, McMurtagh," she said, patting a small Lancashire terrier on the head.

"That's right, boss," snarled the dog. "I ran out of the poodle parlour after one of those perfumed baths, and kept on running."

"Good work," said the Yellow Cat. "Now, boys, time for business. Show me what you've got."

The poker players put down their cards and picked up their pencils and started scribbling.

"Bring them to me, Clive!" said the Yellow Cat.

The cockatoo flapped about gathering up the drawings in his beak and took them to the Yellow Cat.

"Excellent," she purred.

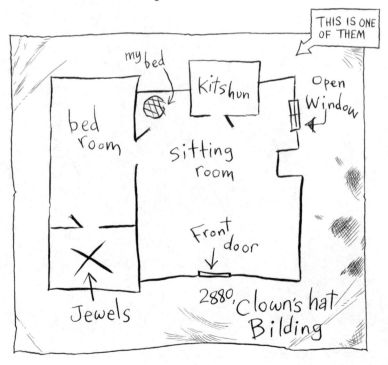

THIS IS ONE OF THEM

my bed

Kitshun

Open Window

bed room

sitting room

bedroom

Front door

Jewels

2880, Clown's hat Bilding

A Penangese lapdog dropped his doggy chew. "I ran off in the park this morning. Mrs. Lloyd threw me a stick and she's still waiting for it. But I'm not going back!"

The Yellow Cat smiled. "If this information is correct, my furry friend," she purred, "then you won't have to!"

Chapter Three

The next morning Ottoline woke up rather later than usual. She put on her Mongolian dressing gown and, stifling a yawn, shuffled down the hallway.

There was a postcard on the doormat.

Greetings From the Empty Quarter

43

AND THIS WAS ON THE BACK

POSTCARD

EMPTY
E 4·02·07
QUARTER

Dearest O, on the trail of the most spectacular camelhair coat to add to our collection. Please try not to spill jam down the front of your mongolian dressing gown, there's a dear. The desert is very hot and it never rains here. Mr. Munroe would love it! Pa sends his love,
Ma.
P.S. Remember to put the umbrella back in the stand and don't stay up too late tonight!
x x x

Miss O. Brown,
Apt. 243,
The Pepperpot Bld.
3rd street,
BIG CITY 3001

Ottoline put the umbrella back in the stand and yawned sleepily.

Then she went to her room to put the postcard in her Postcard collection.

Ottoline loved her Postcard collection even more than her Odd Shoe collection. This was because all the postcards were from her parents.

Ottoline liked looking at the pictures of faraway places on the front of the postcards . . .

THIS IS OTTOLINE'S SECOND COLLECTION

. . . and she loved reading the messages on the back because they made her feel as if her parents weren't so far away.

These are a few of her favourites . . .

Greetings from the Frozen North

Greetings From the Wild West

Greetings
From the
Far East

Greetings
From the
Frozen
South

IF YOU WANT TO
READ THE MESSAGES
ON THE BACK, TURN
THE PAGE →

POSTCARD

Dearest O, Have never seen so many polar bears! The igloo we are staying in is very warm and snug. Please remember to shut the fridge door, there's a love. It's snowing again, don't think Mr. Munroe would like it here. Pa sends his love,
Ma

P.S. On your walks, make sure Mr. Munroe wraps up warm in Pa's raincoat. XXX

FROZEN ★ 13·04·05 ★ NORTH

6248

Miss O. Brown,
Apt. 243,
The Pepperpot Bld.
3rd Street,
BIG CITY 3001

POSTCARD

Dearest O, Finally we have found the Emperor of Heligoland's walking hat! Pa sends his love, lots of love,
Ma.

P.S. Put the top back on the toothpaste!
X X X

WILD ★ 10·06·06 ★ WEST

4¢

Miss O. Brown,
Apt. 243,
The Pepperpot Bld.
3rd Street,
BIG CITY 3001

POSTCARD

Dearest O, ran across some butterfly collectors in the jungle here. Pa was VERY CROSS and took away their butterfly collectors' nets! He sends his love,
Ma

P.S. Tidy your shoe collection, there's a good girl! X X X

FAR
9·11·05
EAST

Miss O. Brown,
Apt. 243,
The Pepperpot Bld.
3rd Street,
BIG CITY 3001

POSTCARD

Dearest O, There are penguins everywhere! Emperor Penguins, King Penguins and Vice-President penguins... The ship is frozen solid in the ice so we're stuck here for a bit. Don't forget to dust the four-spouted teapot collection, my darling. Pa sends his love,
Ma.

P.S. Well done! A diploma in disguise is a very useful thing to have.

FROZEN
★ 29·07·06 ★
SOUTH

°88

Miss O. Brown,
Apt. 243,
The Pepperpot Bld.
3rd Street,
BIG CITY 3001

Ottoline was just putting the postcard in her
collection when Mr. Munroe walked in.
She showed him the postcard.

He looked at it for a long time and then
picked up Ottoline's hairbrush.

"My hair needs brushing?" said Ottoline.

Mr. Munroe nodded. Next to having his own hair brushed, the thing he liked least was brushing someone else's. But he knew that it would make Ottoline feel better, so he did the best he could.

For breakfast that morning Ottoline
had strawberry bagels and apple juice.
Mr. Munroe had porridge and hot chocolate,

which he didn't touch because he was too
busy reading the newspaper.

"It's rude to read at the table," said Ottoline.

After breakfast, as they sat together on the
Beidermeyer sofa, Mr. Munroe showed
Ottoline something he had underlined in the
newspaper in red crayon.

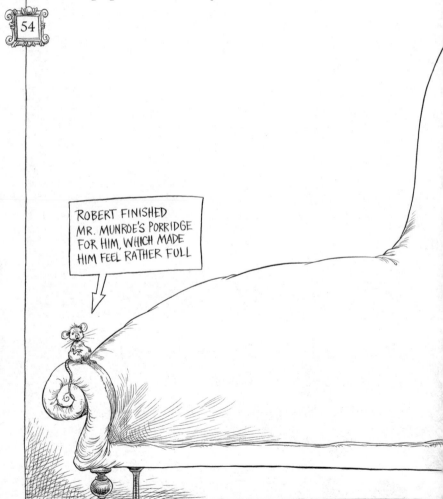

ROBERT FINISHED
MR. MUNROE'S PORRIDGE
FOR HIM, WHICH MADE
HIM FEEL RATHER FULL

THE BIG CITY ENQUIRER

CAT BURGLAR STRIKES AGAIN

By our crime correspondent

Mrs. Loretta Lloyd

Mrs. Loretta Lloyd of the Clown's Hat Building on 3rd Street was the latest victim to fall prey to "The Notorious Cat Burglar". Mrs. Lloyd lost jewellery worth quite a lot in the robbery and was too angry to talk to the *Enquirer* last night but said in a written statement, "I'm so angry!" Police commissioner Ronald Flatfoot admitted, "We are baffled," and appealed to the public to be vigilant and on their guard at all times.

"Mr. Munroe," said Ottoline, "I think it's time you practised your Special Disguises."

Chapter Four

Just then the doorbell rang. Mr. Munroe went to the front door and opened it.

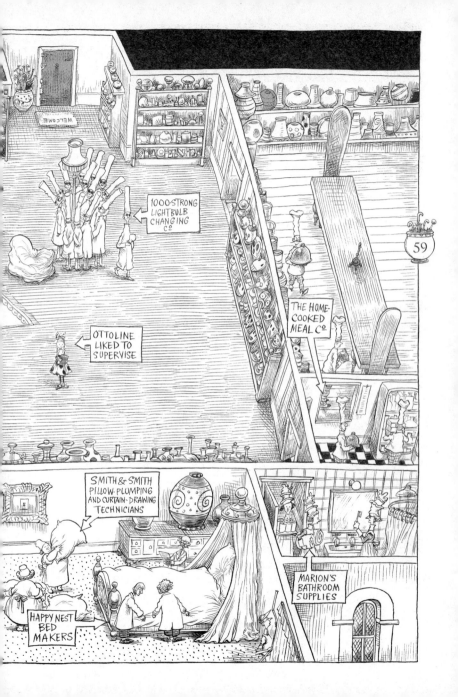

AT TEN O'CLOCK Mr. Munroe came out of
his room and tapped Ottoline on the
shoulder. He was wearing a large, shabby
raincoat.

Ottoline checked the curtains.

"Not now, Mr. Munroe," she said.

Mr. Munroe went back to his room.

AT ELEVEN O'CLOCK Mr. Munroe tapped
Ottoline on the shoulder again. He was
wearing a large, shabby raincoat and a pair
of dark glasses.

Ottoline looked at the door handle.

"Not now, Mr. Munroe," she said.

Mr. Munroe went back to his room.

AT TWELVE O'CLOCK Mr. Munroe coughed loudly. He was wearing a large, shabby raincoat, a pair of dark glasses and the Emperor of Heligoland's hat.

Ottoline examined the toothpaste.

"Not now, Mr. Munroe," she said.

Mr. Munroe went back to his room and
slammed the door.

At lunch . . .

. . . there was very little conversation.

Mr. Munroe was wearing a large shabby raincoat, a pair of dark glasses, the Emperor of Heligoland's hat and an extremely long scarf.

Ottoline inspected her knickers.

"Not now," she said.

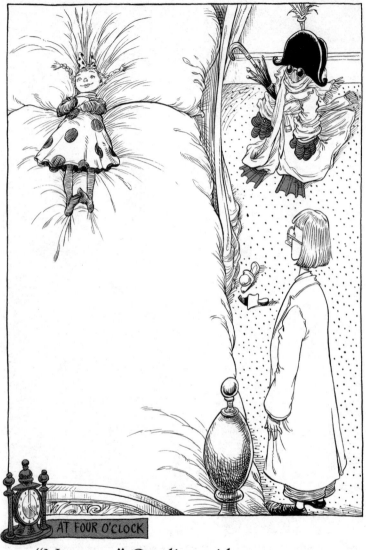

70

AT FOUR O'CLOCK

"Not now," Ottoline said.

AT FIVE O'CLOCK

"Not now."

72

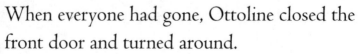

When everyone had gone, Ottoline closed the
front door and turned around.

"Now, Mr. Munroe," she said, "what is it . . . ?"

But Mr. Munroe wasn't there.

Chapter Five

Mr. Munroe
climbed up the
fire escape, which
led to the roof of
the Pepperpot Building.
Every so often, he paused and
listened at the windows.
Mr. Munroe liked listening to the
interesting conversations that went on in
the other apartments. But he didn't tell
Ottoline as he knew she wouldn't approve.

Mr. Munroe stood on the roof of the
Pepperpot Building and thought for a
long time.

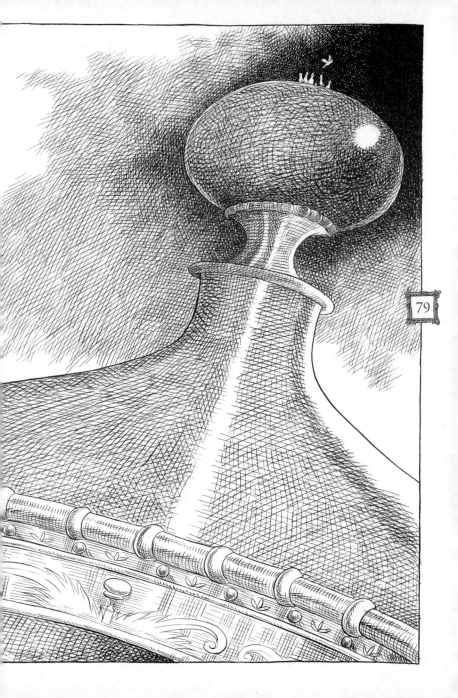

It began to rain ...

. . . very heavily.

82

As he stood in the rain, Mr. Munroe thought about the cold, wet bog in Norway. He

remembered how Ottoline's parents, Professor and Professor Brown, had found him and had invited him to come home with them to the Pepperpot Building.

Professor Brown lent him his nice new raincoat and Professor Brown gave him her sunglasses. The three of them sailed home on the SS *Trondheim*. To avoid unwanted attention they called him Mr. Munroe, although his real name was something in Norwegian that meant "Small-Hairy-Bog-Person".

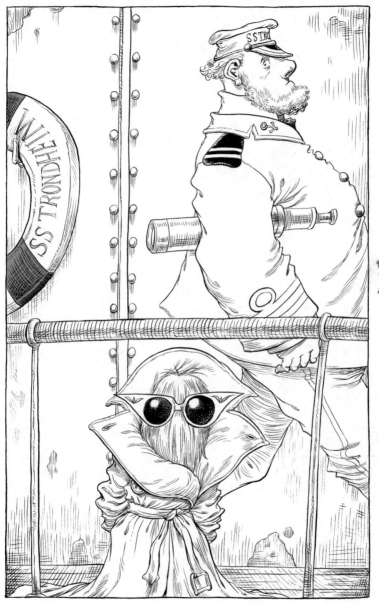

85

From the
moment she
was born,
Ottoline and
Mr. Munroe were
inseparable.

He took her for walks.

He let her brush his hair.

He even let her give him a bath . . .

. . . but only once.

88

But whatever they did, Ottoline's parents
knew that as long as Mr. Munroe was with
her, their daughter would always be safe.

The rain stopped and Mr. Munroe went
down the fire escape. He didn't feel sad
any longer.

He stood on the doormat until he had
stopped dripping.

It felt good to be out of the rain. It felt
good to be far away from the bog in Norway.
It felt good to be living in
the Pepperpot
Building.

Most of all, it felt good to have Ottoline as
his best friend.

Mr. Munroe found Ottoline sitting in the
Beidermeyer
rocking
chair.

OTTOLINE
WAS MAKING
NOTES IN HER
NOTEBOOK

MR. MUNROE
KNEW HOW
RELAXING OTTOLINE
FOUND BRUSHING
HIS HAIR,
ESPECIALLY AFTER
A BUSY DAY

"Would you like me to brush your hair?"
asked Ottoline.

Mr. Munroe nodded.

When she had finished, Ottoline looked at
Mr. Munroe for a long time. Then she looked
at her notebook.

"I've got a clever plan," she said.

Chapter
Six

Late that night, there was a knock on the door of the old warehouse.

"Go away!" yelled the Yellow Cat. "We're closed! Callers by appointment only!"

There was another knock on the door followed by a rather feeble bark.

"All right, all right," complained the Yellow Cat. "Keep your tail on. I'm coming, I'm coming!"

The Yellow Cat opened the door. There was a small hairy dog outside. The small hairy dog handed the Yellow Cat a card.

THIS IS WHAT THE CARD READ

Bimby Bottlenose II
Emperor of Heligoland
Pedigree Norwegian Lapdog

"Lapdog, eh?" said the Yellow Cat. "Then you've come to the right place!" She stepped aside and let him in.

"Look what the cat dragged in," said the Yellow Cat. "Boys, meet Bimby Bottlenose II, Emperor of Heligoland."

The poker players looked up from their game.

"We can call him Nosey," said the Yellow Cat. "Nosey, meet the gang."

RUPE THE FANG

SNARLER McMURTAGH

BUTCH HILBURG

THE SUNDANCE PUP

The gang wagged their tails and made room for Nosey at the table.

"Clive!" said the Yellow Cat. "Make sure the boys don't stay up too late. We've got work tomorrow."

"You're the boss, Boss," squawked the cockatoo.

"So where are you
from, stranger?" said
Rupe the Fang.
Nosey gave him his card.
Rupe looked at it.
"Norway," he said.
"It can get very wet
in Norway."
Nosey nodded and put a
playing card on the table.

"Emperor of Heligoland?"
said Butch Hilburg, chewing
on his doggy treat. "I once
saw the Emperor of
Heligoland. Wore a
splendid hat."
Nosey nodded
and played
another card.

"Care for a doggy treat?" offered
McMurtagh.

Nosey shook his head.

"Don't say much, do you?" McMurtagh
snarled. "What's wrong? Cat got your
tongue?"

"Don't mind him," said the Sundance Pup.
"He's just sore because his last owner took
him to the poodle parlour for a shampoo."

Nosey laid his playing cards on the table.

"Full house!" squawked Clive. "You win!
Time for bed!"

Nosey didn't sleep well in the lapdogs'
basket. Rupe the Fang snored, Snarler
McMurtagh whimpered, Butch Hilburg
chased squirrels in his dreams and the
Sundance Pup
had terrible
wind.

He was just beginning to doze off when the
door opened and the Yellow Cat crept in.

The Yellow Cat opened her bag and
took out an emerald necklace, which
she carefully hid beneath the
floorboards.

Just then, the telephone rang.
The Yellow Cat leaped into the air with
surprise and Clive woke up with a squawk.
"Don't just perch there!" hissed the Yellow
Cat. "Answer it."

Clive picked up the receiver.

"The Lapdog Agency, how may we help you?" he said. "A lapdog? Certainly, madam. We have an excellent selection. Would you care to make an appointment . . . this morning? . . . Yes, I think we can fit you in . . . What time? . . . Now? Well, I suppose . . . let me see . . ."

Just then there was a knock at the door.

"Must I do EVERYTHING myself?" said the Yellow Cat, slinking up the stairs.

Chapter Seven

The Yellow Cat opened the door. An extremely large lady was standing on the doorstep.

"Can I help you?" said the Yellow Cat.

"Mrs. Ursula Jansen-Smith," said the large lady grandly. "I am an incredibly rich but lonely old lady and I'd like a lapdog to take home with me. I've just made an appointment."

Clive put down the telephone.

"Please come in, Mrs. Jansen-Smith," purred the Yellow Cat.

"You can call me Ursula," said the lady.

THE LAMPSHADE FROM PAGE 14

THE EXTREMELY LONG SCARF FROM PAGE 68

THE SUNGLASSES FROM PAGE 62

THE FUR COAT FROM PAGE 20

THE GLOVES FROM PAGE 70

105

"Show time!" said the Yellow Cat.

OLTO   FIFI   Bimby

The lapdogs lined up against the wall. They
held cards with their lapdog names on.

Mrs. Jansen-Smith walked slowly down the line and looked carefully at each lapdog.

"Can I just say what an exquisite hat you're wearing, Mrs. Jansen-Smith?" purred the Yellow Cat, rubbing her paws. "And what a simply stunning outfit."

109

"My hat?" said Mrs. Jansen-Smith. "Do you like it? It was a present from the Emperor of Jutland. And these things? Oh, they're straight from the laundry. I just threw them together!"

Mrs. Jansen-Smith stopped in front of the
last lapdog.

"I'll take this one," she said.

"Excellent choice," purred the Yellow Cat. "Bimby Bottlenose II, Emperor of Heligoland, is a pedigree Norwegian lapdog."

"It can get very wet in Norway," said Mrs. Jansen-Smith thoughtfully. "Send me the bill. Apartment 243, the Pepperpot Building, 3rd Street."

When Mr. Munroe got back to Apartment 243, he found a postcard on the doormat. He picked it up and went to see Ottoline. She was busy writing in her notebook.

Mr. Munroe handed her the postcard.

"Your ribbon has come undone," she said.

IF YOU WOULD LIKE TO SEE THE POSTCARD, TURN THE PAGE

THE TRONDHEIM UMBRELLA FESTIVAL

114

POSTCARD

B. 28·4·07 TRONDHEIM NORWAY

Miss O Brown,
Apt. 243,
The Pepperpot Building
3rd Street,
BIG CITY 3001

Dearest O, Pa has
found some splendid
new umbrellas,
lots of love,
Ma.
× × ×

P.S. Make sure Mr.
Munroe gets to bed!
× × ×

115

"It looks very wet, doesn't it, Mr. Munroe,"
said Ottoline. "Mr. Munroe . . . ?"

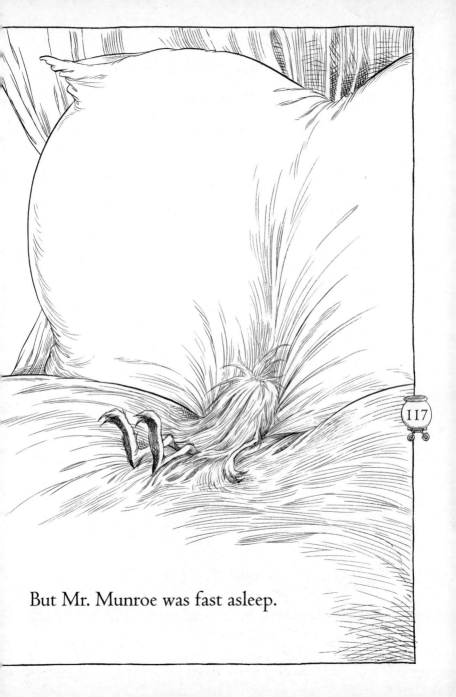

But Mr. Munroe was fast asleep.

117

Chapter Eight

The next morning, Mr. Munroe got up bright and early. He wandered around the apartment . . .

MPERORS' HATS →

EXTREMELY SMALL PAINTINGS

BUTTERFLY COLLECTORS' NETS

119

. . . making careful notes.

243

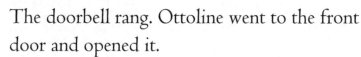

OTTOLINE'S
BOLIVIAN LLAMA-
WOOL ROBE

The doorbell rang. Ottoline went to the front door and opened it.

"We're not too early, I hope," said the chef
from the Home-Cooked Meal Company.

"No," said Ottoline. "There's lots to get
ready."

For breakfast, Ottoline had waffles and maple syrup. Mr. Munroe had porridge and hot chocolate, which he didn't touch because he was busy finishing his notes.

"It's rude to write at the table," said
Ottoline.

After breakfast, as they sat on the Beidermeyer pouffe, Mr. Munroe showed Ottoline his notes.

She looked at them for a long time and then she said, "Good work, Mr. Munroe."

ROBERT CARRYING A PIECE OF LEFTOVER WAFFLE

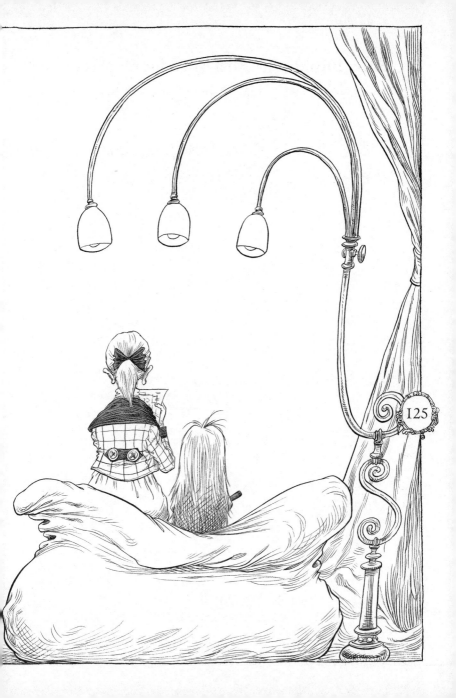

Then Ottoline brushed Mr. Munroe's hair . . .

. . . very
thoroughly . . .

. . . and tied a ribbon in it.

She kissed him on the forehead.

"You're very brave," she said. "Now you'd better go."

Mr. Munroe nodded.

Ottoline waited until Mr. Munroe had gone and then she walked to Gruberman's Korean Theatre. She carefully unfolded a poster and stuck it to the lamp post.

LOST

A Pedigree Norwegian
Lapdog
answers to the name of
Bimby Bottlenose II
Emperor of Heligoland
much missed by his loving owner
LARGE REWARD
Contact Mrs. Jansen-Smith Apartment 243
THE PEPPERPOT BUILDING · 3rd street · B.C.

129

Mr. Munroe knocked on the warehouse door.

"Hiya, Nosey," the Yellow Cat said. "You're a fast worker."

REPAIRED
BUTTERFLY
COLLECTOR'S
NET

133

IF YOU WOULD LIKE TO
SEE THE PIECE OF PAPER,
TURN THE PAGE

The gang crowded round.

"OK, show me what you've got," said the
Yellow Cat.

Nosey handed her a piece of paper.

Apartment 243, the Pepperpot Building

Emperors' hats

extremely small paintings

sofa

NOTHING interesting HERE!

rocking Chair

armchair

Collections

odd shoe collection

dressing table

Fire Escape

Wardrobe

Window

Window

Mrs. Jansen-Smith's Bedroom

frontdoor

WELCOME

Umbrellas

collections

Dining

Sitting
room

pouffe

collections

room

Kitchen

pots →

bathroom

bed →

Jewels are in
this
cupboard

window

ARMPIT HAIR

135

The Yellow Cat looked at the drawing for a long time. "Excellent work, Nosey," she purred as she left the room. "Excellent."

"Welcome back," snarled Snarler McMurtagh. "Feeling lucky?"

Nosey nodded and sat down at the table with the other lapdogs. Butch Hilburg dealt the cards.

"Didn't take you long to give your owner the slip," said Rupe the Fang. "Very careless, some of these ladies."

Nosey nodded again and played a card.

"So is the rumour true?" Butch said to Rupe. "Are you thinking of going back to Mrs. Lloyd?"

"What if I am?" replied Rupe. "Sometimes a dog just wants a quiet lap to sit on for the rest of his days. I'm getting too old for a life on the run."

"I miss Mrs. Armstrong," said the Sundance Pup with a sniff.

Nosey put his last card on the table.

"Full house!" squawked Clive the cockatoo. "You win!"

Chapter Nine

That night, as the lapdogs slept in their basket, the Yellow Cat tiptoed up the stairs and out of the door without a sound.

Butch Hilburg turned over and thumped his tail and Rupe the Fang licked his chops noisily and got comfortable before he started snoring again.

Mr. Munroe
gently
removed
Snarler
McMurtagh's
front paws from
his head and
quietly climbed
out of the basket.

Reaching up, he tugged his
bow undone and let the ribbon fall to
the floor. Then he tiptoed across to the
corner of the room.

Mr. Munroe carefully
tilted the loose floor-
board. It gave a
small creak.

Clive woke up and saw Mr. Munroe with the loot. He let out a piercing screech: "Stop, thief!"

But Mr. Munroe was prepared.

142

He tied up Clive firmly with the polka-dot
ribbon, wrapping it once around his legs,
twice around his wings and three times
around his beak. He then tied a bow in it and
pulled it tight.

"Umph! Umph! Umph!" said Clive.

Mr. Munroe then sat down at the table,
picked up the telephone and started to dial . . .

144

Just then the doorbell rang and the lapdogs
woke up.

"What time is it?" snarled Snarler
McMurtagh.

"I was having a wonderful dream about
squirrels," yawned Butch Hilburg.

"What's that terrible smell?" asked the
Sundance Pup.

"Umph! Umph! Umph!" said Clive the
cockatoo.

The doorbell rang again.

Mr. Munroe climbed the stairs and opened the door.

Four ladies came in. They looked strangely
familiar.

Mr. Munroe presented each of them with
their stolen jewels.

"Time to come home, you naughty, naughty
boy," said Mrs. Armstrong.

The Sundance Pup wagged his tail.

"Walkies!" said Mrs. Lloyd.

Rupe the Fang barked excitedly.

"Here, boy!" said Mrs. Wilson, and Butch
Hilburg rushed up to her.

"Come to Mummy!" cooed Pinky
Neugerbauer. "My little
poodle-doodle!"

"You'll never
take me alive!"
snarled Snarler
McMurtagh.

151

152

The ladies thanked Mr. Munroe
for all his help. They promised
not to press charges as long as
the lapdogs behaved
themselves.

When they had gone, Mr. Munroe locked the
door of the old warehouse.

Then he picked up Clive the cockatoo and
set off towards the Pepperpot Building.

Chapter Ten

The Yellow Cat climbed in through the window of Apartment 243 and looked around.

With one gloved paw, she reached into her bag and took out Mr. Munroe's drawing. She examined it carefully, then crept on tiptoe towards Ottoline's bedroom.

pening the door a crack, the Yellow Cat
pped inside. She didn't make a sound.

hen she sneaked over to the cupboard and
owly opened it . . .

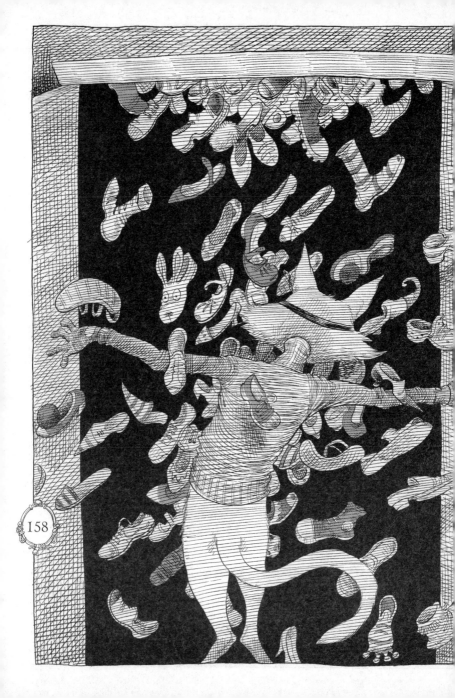

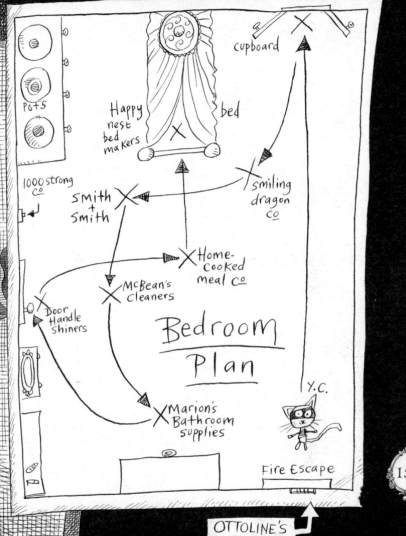

OTTOLINE'S NOTEBOOK

Suddenly a light flicked on.

With a startled miaow the Yellow Cat sprang to her feet and dashed for the door.

Dodging a collapsing tower of neatly folded cardigans . . .

Ducking an avalanche of perfectly plumped pillows . . .

. . . she leaped over the vacuum cleaner and
the floor mop . . .

. . . and swerved under the swishing shower
curtain.

The Yellow Cat struggled to get a grip on the shiny door knob. She was about to try for the window when . . .

. . . half a dozen home-cooked custard pies sailed through the air towards her . . .

. . . and an incredibly large bear jumped out of the neatly made bed.

"Mrs. Jansen-Smith!" yowled the Yellow Cat.

163

The bear caught her in a big bear hug.
"Curses!" hissed the Yellow Cat.

"Hello," said Ottoline. "You didn't really think you'd get away with it, did you?"

"Tell me, how did you do it?" asked the Yellow Cat.

"Simple – with the help of my friends," said Ottoline, "and a clever plan."

OTTOLINE'S
MADAGASCAN
MOHAIR
DRESSING
GOWN →

Just then the doorbell rang.

It was Mr. Munroe and the Pet Police.

"We'll take it from here, miss," said the
Pet Policeman to Ottoline. "We've been
after these two for quite a while."

"What will happen to them?" asked
Ottoline.

"They'll be going away for a very long
time," said the policeman. "To a petting zoo
in the country."

"Curses!" said Clive the cockatoo.

Ottoline turned to Mr. Munroe and gave him a hug. "I'm very, very proud of you," she said.

Mr. Munroe nodded and Ottoline, who knew Mr. Munroe better than anyone else in the world, was sure that he was smiling.

167

Just then Ottoline saw the postcard on the doormat. She picked it up. It was from her parents.

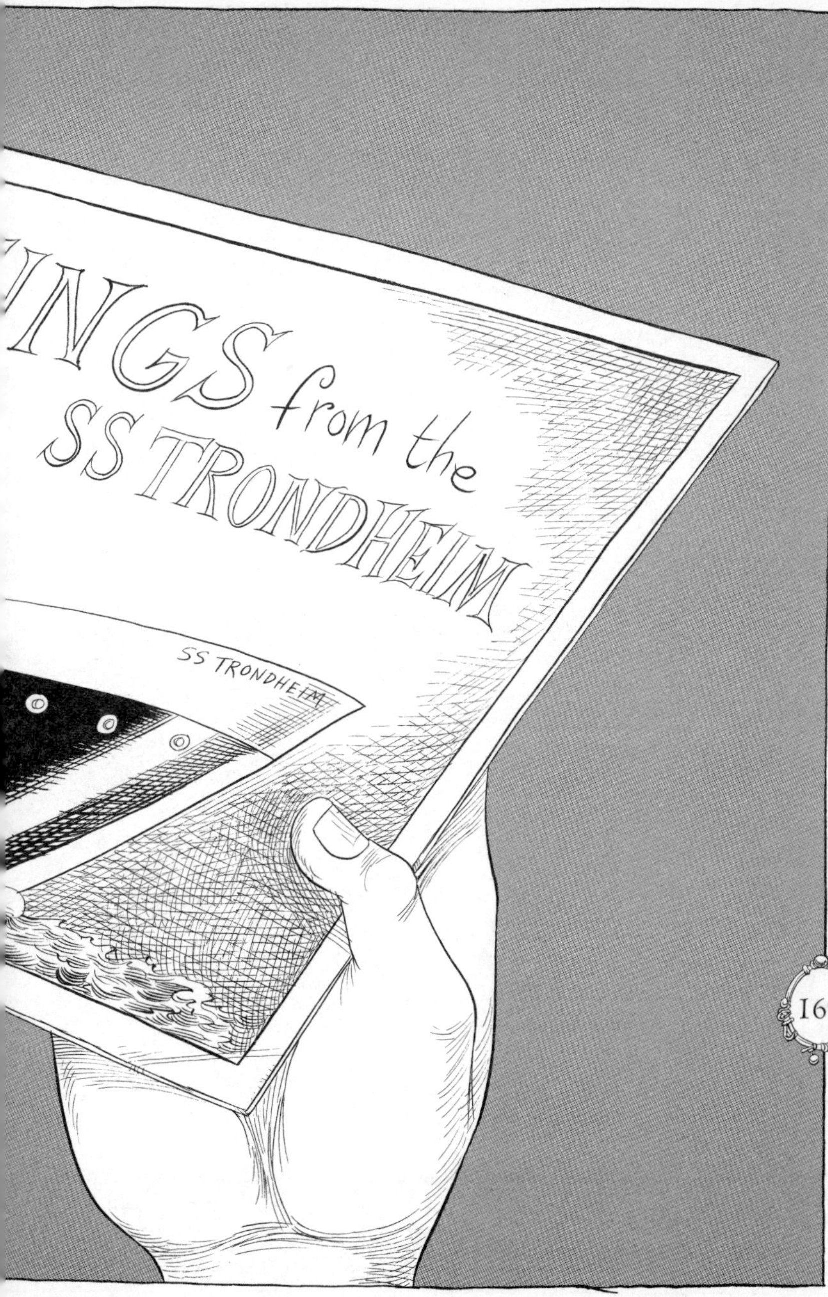
INGS from the
SS TRONDHEIM
SS TRONDHEIM

Dearest O,

we are on our way home. Pa and I can't wait to see you,

lots of love,

Ma.

P.S. Tell that nice bear he can stay as long as he wants.

P.P.S. Please clear up those custardpies, there's a good girl! XXX

Miss O. Brown,

Apartment 243,

The Pepperpot Bld.

3rd Street,

BIG CITY 3001

171

ACADEMY OF SUBTERFUGE

THIS IS TO CERTIFY THAT

Mr. Monroe

IS A CERTIFIED MASTER OF DISGUISE

PROFESSOR MYSTERY
M.D.

First published 2007 by Macmillan Children's Books

This edition published 2015 by Macmillan Children's Books
an imprint of Pan Macmillan
20 New Wharf Road, London N1 9RR
Associated companies throughout the world
www.panmacmillan.com

ISBN: 978-0-330-45028-7

Printed and bound by CPI Group (UK) Ltd, Croydon CR0 4YY

7 9 8 6